PIC

PICTURE BOOK STUDIO USA

M. L. Miller

DIZZY FROM FOOLS

Illustrated by Eve Tharlet

"Why can't a *girl* ever be the Court Fool?" the Princess asked her mother one day.

"Because," said the Queen, "in this land only the boys grow up to be Fools."

"But why?" asked the Princess.

"Because it's always been that way," explained her mother. "From the beginning of time."

"But it's such a nice thing to be," said the Princess. "You don't have to be dignified or wear heavy robes. You can be funny and wise – and take peoples' minds off their problems. A *girl* could do that."

"Don't let your father hear you say that," warned the Queen. "You know what a temper he has."

Now it so happened that before long the Court Fool ran away to Medical School to become a doctor. The King was very upset, but he knew you could never tell what a Fool would do next. So he decided to hold a contest and pick a new and even better Court Fool. Messengers were sent far and wide to spread the word.

And from every corner of the land came men of every size, shape, and age to try out for the job.

There were Fools riding pigs, and Fools with striped sceptres, and Fools with the giggles and bells on their toes. There was one who sang all his words, and a Fool with a fence, and a Fool covered from head to foot with bright autumn leaves – who played on a tiny tuba, then turned double cartwheels all over the throne room. Such a trick was unheard of.

Then he suddenly stopped before the King with a riddle.

"Everybody bows to the King," said the Fool, bowing grandly. "But when does the King bow?"

"The King bows to no one!" declared the great ruler. "There can be no such thing."

"Oh, no?" said the Fool.

"Well, when *does* the King bow?" asked the King, who liked a good riddle.

"When he looks in the mirror," the Fool replied.

"Stuff and nonsense!" said the King, pretending to be
gruffer than he really was. He was testing this Fool.
"And have you another?"

"What is so much better because it isn't all there?"

"Such things cannot be!" said the King, gruffer than before.
"Well, what *is*?"

"Swiss cheese."

"Oh, enough of you, Fool," said the King, who had never
missed two riddles in a row before. But he was smiling
secretly to himself, for he knew a good Fool when he saw one.

Then the King sat back and gave all the others their chance
to perform, watching until he was dizzy from Fools.

Then he ordered everybody out of the throne room while he decided who would be the next Court Fool. But that didn't take much deciding! He already knew it could only be the Fool in bright leaves. But the King loved building up to announcements.

However, when he called everyone back in, the winner was nowhere to be found. They searched high and low in the palace, they searched down the roads and into the woods, but he had disappeared. The King was so disgusted he sent all the others home and scowled and stormed through the palace for hours.

That night the Princess, seeing how unhappy her father was, tried to comfort him. But he was still fuming, "The best Fool in the land and he disappears just like *that*," – snapping his fingers.

"I'm sorry, Father," said the Princess. "But I could pretend to be Court Fool for a while and cheer you up."

"Nonsense, Daughter!" growled the King. "Such things cannot be."

"But why?"

"Why?" he exploded. "Because *here* only the boys grow up to be Fools! It's always been that way – from the beginning of time. The *King* has spoken!...

"Now you just forget about such things," he said a little more gently, "and get a good night's sleep. It's been a difficult day."

"Very well, Father," she said, kissing him goodnight on the forehead.

Then she promptly turned double cartwheels out the door
and down the long hallway and vanished.

The King was thunderstruck. Then, in spite of himself, he burst into laughter at the thought of his daughter's charade, and raced down the corridors calling after the best Fool of all to return and lighten his heart.

And so she did.

Copyright © 1985, Neugebauer Press USA Inc.
Published in USA by Picture Book Studio USA,
an imprint of Neugebauer Press USA Inc.
Distributed by Alphabet Press, Natick, MA.
Distributed in Canada by Vanwell Publishing, St. Catharines, Ont.
Published in U.K. by Neugebauer Press Publishing Ltd., London.
All rights reserved.
Printed in Austria.

LIBRARY OF CONGRESS CATALOGING IN PUBLICATION DATA

Miller, M. L.
Dizzy from fools.

Summary: A young girl becomes a court jester despite
her father's objections.
[1. Sex role–Fiction] I. Tharlet, Eve, ill. II. Title.
PZ7.M627Di   1985   [E]   85-9390
ISBN 0-88708-004-9